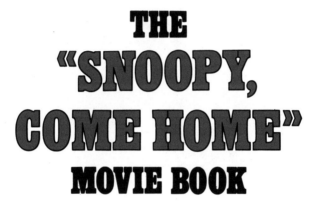

THE "SNOOPY, COME HOME" MOVIE BOOK

THE "SNOOPY, COME HOME" MOVIE BOOK

CHARLES M. SCHULZ

Holt, Rinehart and Winston

New York   Chicago   San Francisco

Printed in the United States of America

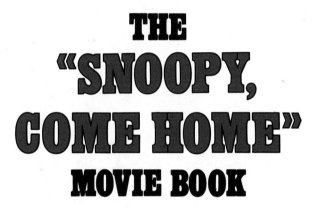

She had not been feeling well and she had been in the hospital room for almost three weeks. Now she was very lonely.

Her parents had given her several books and a small doll to play with, but somehow these things did not cure her loneliness.

She recalled a friend from long ago and she decided to write a letter to this friend. It was only a short
note, but she hoped that it might bring her friend to
visit.

Across town, many miles away, another little girl, completely different in appearance, was building a sand castle on the beach. She had rather wild, funny looking hair and she had three freckles on each cheek. Her name was Peppermint Patty.

The friend who was playing with her was Snoopy and because Peppermint Patty was not always too sure about some things, she never realized this funny looking kid was really a dog. When Snoopy had gone to the beach that morning, he had put on a nice little pair of bathing trunks and a floppy beach hat.

They ran down to
the edge of the water and
splashed along the shore.

A huge wave came
in and toppled
them in
the sand.

They rolled in the sand, but instead of being frightened, they merely laughed. They were having a wonderful time.

"You know, Snoopy," said Peppermint Patty, "everyone should be allowed to have at least one day out of the week at the beach. Sometimes it's nice to lie in the sun and just do nothing. Of course, it's better if you're with someone you like. You kind of like me, don't you, Snoopy?" Then she suggested that they meet again at the same place tomorrow. "If you come," said Peppermint Patty, "I'll bring a picnic lunch. We'll have sandwiches and cookies and root beer, potato chips and everything, ok?" This sounded great to Snoopy, for there was nothing in the world that he loved better than a good picnic. So the two friends agreed that they would meet on the beach the following day.

Back home, Charlie Brown, who was Snoopy's owner, looked out of the living room window, saw Snoopy returning home.

"That dog," he said. "I don't know what I'm going to do with him. He seems to come and go as he pleases, but I have to stay home and fix his supper."

He went into the kitchen, opened the cupboard, got out a can of dog food and began to open it with a can opener.

The can opener slipped, however, and he yelled
"Ow" as it nicked his finger.

He was grumbling angrily to himself as he carried the dish of dog food out into the backyard. "All right, it's supper time. Come and get your supper." Then he showed his bandaged finger to Snoopy and he asked him, "Do you see this finger? I cut it opening a stupid can of dog food for your stupid supper. I hope you appreciate it. Besides, it wasn't even a finger, it was a thumb!" He was so mad about everything that he began to lecture Snoopy on the terrible way he had been acting lately.

He said, "Don't forget that I'm the one who feeds you. I'm the one who takes care of you. Just remember, without me, you'd be nothing. Everything you have, you have because of me. Even that collar around your neck. Why, I remember the day I went out and bought that collar with money I had worked for and had saved."

This didn't seem to bother Snoopy at all, for he simply reached up, unhooked the collar and handed it back to Charlie Brown.

All poor Charlie Brown could do was gaze up into the sky and say, "I hate it when he does that."

The next day was bright and sunny and Peppermint Patty arrived at the beach early. She spread a blanket on the sand, put down a picnic basket with all the good things in it and set the portable radio nearby. Then she opened the colorful beach umbrella, stuck it into the sand, and sat down to wait for Snoopy.

When Snoopy came out of his doghouse that morning, he had all sorts of things gathered together which he had planned to take to the beach. He had a huge surfboard, some bath towels, a picnic basket of his own and all of the things which a person likes to have when he plans to spend a whole day at the beach.

Things didn't work out as he had planned, however. As he was approaching the beach area, he passed a new sign which evidently had just been put up. It said, "NO DOGS ALLOWED ON THIS BEACH."

Before he knew it, Snoopy was being booted back to where he had come from, and all of his belongings were thrown on top of him. Poor Peppermint Patty had no idea, of course, that this had happened and when Snoopy did not show up, all she could do was shake her head, sigh and say to herself, "I think I've been stood up."

Snoopy had a very nice little pal whom he referred to as his "Friend of Friends." His name was Woodstock; he was a little yellow bird and he would frequently serve as Snoopy's secretary because he was a very good typist.

Snoopy was so mad about not being allowed on the beach that he decided to write a letter to the local newspaper.

After Woodstock finished typing the letter, Snoopy signed it with his paw print.

To the Editor
Dear Sir:
    It has come to our attention that a new sign has been posted on the beach which says that no dogs will be allowed there-on.
    Therefore I am writing to protest this policy.
    Very Sincerely Yours,

Woodstock then put the letter in an envelope,
and flew away in his usual upside-down manner...

. . . bumping into things but eventually getting the letter to the mailbox.

Now that he could not spend the day at the beach, Snoopy decided to join Charlie Brown and Sally who were going down to the library. Sally was Charlie Brown's younger sister and she really didn't care about doing things like this because she always thought it was a waste of time. "I know why you want me to go to the library," she said. "You're just trying to trick me into learning how to read, that's what you are trying to do."

But Charlie Brown cautioned her to be quiet as they went into the building. "Libraries are very dignified places," he warned, "and you are not supposed to cause any commotion."

Snoopy had never been in a library before, and he was fascinated by the rows of books. He even leaned forward once and tasted one, but discovered that it was kind of bland. Then he found a little book called *The Bunnies* and he took it over to the library table and started to read it. It was just about the funniest book he had ever read. He started to laugh and then he began to pound the table and laugh harder and harder.

The next thing he knew he had been forcibly ejected from the library and had landed on the sidewalk right next to a sign which read "NO DOGS ALLOWED IN LIBRARY."

It had been an exhausting morning so Snoopy went back to the doghouse and fell sound asleep on the top where he always did his best resting. Charlie Brown had found a letter in the mailbox for him and awakened him and told him the letter was his.

As soon as he glanced at it, Snoopy knew that he was going to have to leave.

This was very puzzling to Charlie Brown and when he saw Snoopy quickly pack a small suitcase and put his dog dish on his head, he said, "Where are you going, what are you doing, why are you packed? Are you going someplace?" Snoopy called to his little friend Woodstock who came up and the two of them bid Charlie Brown a quick good-bye and raced off.

Now Charlie Brown was almost panicky, "Where is he going?" he shouted. Then in dismay he cried, "I never know what's going on."

The journey that Snoopy and Woodstock took was a very strange one. The first time they tried to get on a bus they were promptly ejected.

They walked for several hours and finally came to a small stream.

While Snoopy cooled his tired feet in the water, Woodstock, being a great craftsman with twigs and branches, made a beautiful little raft.

However, when Snoopy stepped onto the raft with his luggage, the whole thing sank.

In the meantime, Charlie Brown was worrying about the disappearance of his dog. "He's gone," said Charlie Brown. "He's gone, and I don't know why."

"You say he got this letter and then he just took off?" asked Linus. "What did the letter say?"

Charlie Brown opened the letter which Snoopy had received and read it out loud. "Dear Snoopy, I have been in the hospital for three weeks and am very lonely. Could you come to see me? Love, Lila."

"Lila!" said Linus. "Who in the world is Lila?"

All Charlie Brown could say was, "If I don't find out who Lila is, I'll go crazy!"

Now, somewhere along the way, Snoopy and Woodstock became lost. When you are lost, one of the best ways to find out how to get back to going the right way is simply to ask someone. A dark-haired little girl was sitting in her backyard playing with a small shovel and pail. Snoopy went over to her and tipped his dog dish which he wore as a hat, hoping that by appearing very friendly the girl might be able to offer them some help.

Instead, she leaped up, grabbed Snoopy around
the neck, ran across the yard with him, and shouted,
"Hey, Ma! I found a stray dog."

Then, before he knew it, Snoopy was tied near the back of the house with a huge rope which even Woodstock could not get untied. While Woodstock was trying desperately to rescue Snoopy, the same little girl swooped down upon him with a net and captured him too. "Hey, Ma, I also found a lost bird!" she shouted.

She went inside and put poor Woodstock in a cage and she said "This is great! Now I have two pets. A sheepdog and a parrot!" Then she went out into the backyard and talked to Snoopy. "Mom said I can keep you, puppy. But if I'm going to have a dog, I think I'll have to give you a good name. How about Rex? That would be a great name! I'm going to dress you up in some nice doll clothes and we'll play tea party. How does that sound, Rex?" Snoopy looked silly sitting in the little dress and a fancy hat and all he could think of was how he was ever going to get away from this girl and find his way to the hospital where Lila was waiting for him.

All of a sudden, he leaped up and ran out of the open door, raced through the living room, grabbed the bird cage which held Woodstock and escaped from the house.

You have never seen an animal and a bird run so fast!

On the next day,
Snoopy and Woodstock
finally arrived at the hospital.

Naturally, there was a sign outside that said "NO DOGS ALLOWED IN HOSPITAL" so they had to sneak in very quietly. They found the room where Lila was, and when she saw her friend had returned, she cried out, "Snoopy, I knew you'd come," and she hugged him close to her. At last, she was happy again and her loneliness disappeared.

DOCTOR:
PATIENT:

Charlie Brown, of course, still did not feel much
better. "If we don't find out what happened to Snoopy,
I think I'll go crazy!"

"Well," said Linus, "If you'll be a little patient, maybe I can conduct a private investigation."

"Just what I need," said Charlie Brown. "A blanket-carrying Sherlock Holmes!"

Linus dialed a number on the telephone. "Hello, Daisy Hill Puppy Farm? I'm calling in regard to a dog named Snoopy. Uh huh, that's right. Charlie Brown. Yes. Oh, really? Wow! I bet he never knew that. That explains a lot of things."

He ran outside, and called to Charlie Brown. "I have news about Snoopy. I think I know just what happened."

"Well, tell me," said Charlie Brown. "Don't just stand there! Tell me!"

"The first thing I did in my investigation was to call the Daisy Hill Puppy Farm. I found out something that will amaze you. In fact, I hesitate to tell you. Are you ready for a shock?"

Clunk! Charlie Brown fell over backwards.

"He wasn't ready for a shock," said Linus.

"How can I tell you something that will shock you if you pass out before I can tell you?"

"I'm sorry," said Charlie Brown. "I've been passing out a lot lately."

"Well, anyway," said Linus, "here's what I found out. You are not Snoopy's original owner!"

Clunk! Charlie Brown fell over again.

"Good grief," said Linus. "I don't think I can stand this for very long."

After Charlie Brown had recovered, Linus continued: "You bought Snoopy in the month of October, right? According to the records of the Daisy Hill Puppy Farm, Snoopy was bought by another family in August. This family had a little girl named Lila. Snoopy and Lila loved each other very much, but they had to move, and the family decided they just couldn't keep Snoopy so they returned him. You got a used dog, Charlie Brown."

"But what about the letter?"

"Well," said Linus, "he had evidently tried to forget her, but when she wrote to him, he felt that he had to go back to the hospital to visit her."

"I bet he wishes he was still her dog instead of mine," said Charlie Brown.

In the hospital, Lila, Snoopy and Woodstock were playing games. This was the happiest that Lila had been in a long time. She seemed to feel well for the first time in many months, but she knew that if Snoopy were to leave again now, she would not be able to stand her loneliness.

"I think your coming to visit me saved me, Snoopy, but now you have to go home again, don't you? Well, you can go to your new owner if you want to, but I wish you'd stay."

Snoopy really hated to go. He still loved little Lila and he knew how sick she had been and how she had missed him, but he also remembered that he had a wonderful life with Charlie Brown and he just did not see how he could stay with Lila. They said good-bye, and Snoopy and Woodstock left the room.

When they reached the sidewalk, Snoopy looked up and saw Lila standing in the window. He couldn't resist running back upstairs for one last hug.

Then Lila said, "Snoopy, I just cannot let you go. Promise me you'll come back. I know that you have to return for a little while to settle your affairs, but please promise me you'll come back."

Now Snoopy had a real problem. He knew that he had promised to return to Lila and that he was going to have to leave his old way of life. He began to make out a list of his belongings which he decided to leave to all the children in the neighborhood who had been good to him.

When Charlie Brown asked him what he was doing, he showed him the list.

"I, Snoopy, being of sound mind, do bequeath to Charlie Brown, my previous owner . . ."

"Previous owner," cried Charlie Brown. "Don't tell me you're going to leave? Does this mean that you're going back to Lila for good?" Snoopy had to admit this was true.

That night at the huge farewell party in his honor, Snoopy felt a sadness unlike anything he had ever felt before.

Lucy stood up in front of everyone and said, "It is with heavy hearts that we are gathered to say good-bye to our friend Snoopy. He leaves us in the prime of his life. He wasn't much of a dog, but who is? We shall miss our furry friend. At this time I want to offer this gesture of friendship, a little gift for old time's sake." And she gave him a small package.

Then each of the children came to the head of
the table and said a small farewell. It was all very
touching, for they had been together for a long time
and loved each other very much. The last person to
approach the head of the table was Snoopy's owner,
Charlie Brown, and he found that he could not say a
word. He stood with his head bowed, and then handed
Snoopy his going-away present.

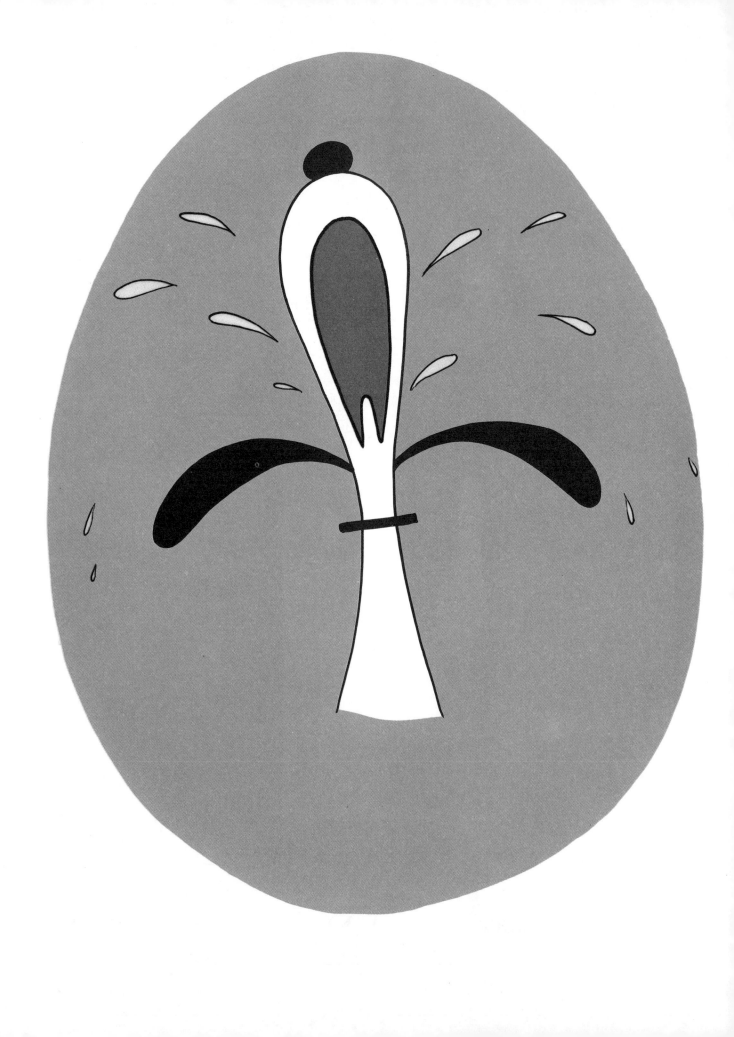

Then it was time for Snoopy to open the presents...

...and when he did he discovered that they were all alike.

Now it was time to leave. Woodstock had thought that he was going along, but when he found out that he couldn't, he was crushed.

One last farewell between friends and they parted.

Now Charlie Brown felt worse than he had ever felt before in his life. "I don't know why we are always having to say good-bye to friends," he said.

"Why can't we get all the people together in the world that we really like and then just stay together? I guess that wouldn't work. Someone would leave. Someone always leaves and then we have to say good-bye. I hate good-byes. I know what I need."

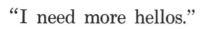

"I need more hellos."

This had been a sad journey for Snoopy, but he was doing what he felt he had to do. He found the address of the apartment where Lila lived.

Then he walked slowly up the stairs to the entrance. He rang the bell of her apartment, and as he waited for her to answer he looked around. Then he saw it.

A sign that said "NO DOGS ALLOWED IN BUILDING."

Suddenly, he knew he was saved! He had done the right thing, and yet he did not have to stay.

Lila came to the door . . .

... and Snoopy pointed to the sign.

Lila understood and so did her cat who had appeared at the door and jumped into her arms. Snoopy shook hands with the cat, and then with Lila, and rushed down the steps.

Charlie Brown and his friends were happy beyond belief when they saw Snoopy return.

They held hands and danced around him and took him on their shoulders and carried him home.

That evening, Snoopy lay on his doghouse completely contented. He felt he had done the right thing toward everyone, and yet he also had what he wanted for himself. His conscience was clear, his stomach was full, and he was home.